The Greedy Man in the Moon

Retold by Rick Rossiter

Illustrated by Dick Smolinski

In memory of my mother Virginia,
and for my father Warren.

Extra special thanks for the help
and guidance from my wife Lee Anne Rossiter,
mentor Arne Nixon, storytelling coach Dan Pessano,
and editor Laura Belgrave.

Published by Riverbank Press
801 94th Avenue North, St. Petersburg, Florida 33702

Copyright © 1994 by Riverbank Press,
a division of PAGES, Inc.

Printed in the United States of America

2 4 6 8 10 9 7 5 3 1

ISBN 0-87406-708-1

The story behind **The Greedy Man in the Moon**

The Greedy Man in the Moon is a folktale that was first told many centuries ago in China. It has passed through the countries of Japan, Korea, Tibet, the United States, and certainly many more. In each country the story found a home, and in each country the story continued to travel as listeners became storytellers by reshaping the tale from pictures in their imaginations. This magic circle of storytellers and listeners, and listeners who become storytellers, is the lifeblood of folktales and of storytelling itself.

The Greedy Man in the Moon is a special story for reading, and an extra special story for telling. After you have read it three times, close your eyes and think about the story events in the order in which they take place. Next, practice fifteen or twenty minutes in front of a mirror, then find a younger child or family member and tell the story. If you don't remember every detail, good! Storytellers do not memorize stories. And if you make a few mistakes, good! All storytellers make mistakes. With experience, you will learn to ignore them.

Though storytelling can be a lifelong adventure with more stories to tell than stars in the sky, the reader need tell only one story to join this magic circle.

So now it is time to begin. . . .

Once, many years ago near a Chinese village, a boy lived with his mother at the edge of a forest. They were very poor, but generous with whatever they had.

The boy loved the forest and each day when his chores were done, he would go hiking. One afternoon he came upon a sparrow lying on the ground. The boy picked it up and said, "Oh, little bird, you have hurt your leg. I shall take you home."

When he returned to his house, he showed the bird to his mother.

"It has broken its leg," she said. "We must take care of it." She carefully wrapped the bird's injured leg, while the boy gathered seeds for it to eat.

Each morning they gave it food and water, and each day the sparrow grew stronger.

At the end of one month's time the bird was fully healed. The boy gently took it to an open window and said, "Little sparrow, it is time for you to return to the forest." He stood with his mother and watched it fly off.

But the next morning, as they ate breakfast, the sparrow returned. In its beak it held a single seed. Then the bird did something strange. It dropped the seed on the window sill near the boy, and spoke! "I wish to thank you for helping me. Plant this special seed and see what grows." And then it flew away.

The boy planted the seed and cared for it each day. In three days' time a tiny melon plant began to sprout. In one week's time the melon plant had grown nearly full size, and it had one golden blossom in its center. In two weeks' time a single ripe, plump melon hung from the vine.

The boy picked the melon up, and as he held it in his hands, it split open. Inside he found a gold coin! When he took the coin into his hand, a second coin appeared in its place. He picked up the second coin, and a third appeared. Each time he removed a coin, another appeared. Suddenly, the boy and his mother were very, very rich.

As it happened, there also lived a greedy, mean-hearted man in the same village. The man spent his days looking for ways to fill his pockets with gold. When he heard that the boy and his mother had suddenly become rich, he quickly paid them a visit.

"It is wonderful that you have all this gold," the greedy man said. "How is it that you came upon such good fortune?"

The boy and his mother told the greedy man every detail of the story. When they were done, the greedy man thought to himself, "So that is their little secret. Well, no one deserves riches more than I! I will go find my own bird."

The next morning, he went into the forest, looking for a bird with a broken leg. He searched and searched, but soon ran out of patience. So he picked up a stone, took careful aim, and whack! He knocked a sparrow from the limb of a tree. The sparrow fell to the ground, its leg broken.

The greedy man walked over, looked at the bird, and said, "Oh, poor thing! Did you hurt yourself? How lucky you are that I came upon you. Don't worry. I will give you very, very, very good care."

He took the bird home and put it in a cage. Each morning he gave it food and water, and each day the bird grew stronger.

At the end of one month's time the sparrow was fully healed. The greedy man held it near a window and said, "All right, little bird, it's time for you to get out of here now."

The little sparrow looked at the greedy man for a moment, then flew off.

The greedy man stayed up all night waiting for the bird to return and dreaming of the things he would buy with more gold coins than even he could imagine.

With the morning sun, the sparrow returned with a single seed in its beak. The bird dropped the seed onto the window sill and said to the greedy man, "I wish you to have something special. Plant this seed and you will see what grows." And then it flew away.

Quickly, the greedy man planted that seed. He tended it each day and on the third day a tiny melon plant began to sprout. By the end of one week's time, a dozen golden blossoms filled its center.

"Ha ha! Twelve blossoms!" the greedy man laughed. "The boy only got one! Now we shall see who becomes the richest in all of the land!"

The plant was very different in another way, too. As the blossoms turned to melons, the long runners of the plant grew straight up into the air instead of growing along the ground. In two weeks' time, the plant was taller than the greedy man's house, and the ripe melons hung from the very top.

"It must be a very rich melon plant indeed," the greedy man said. "And now, I shall harvest my little golden crop of melons."

He stepped onto the vine and began to climb. With each step, the plant grew taller. He climbed and climbed until finally he reached the first melon.

He broke it open at once, but instead of a gold coin, he found nothing but a worm. "A fat worm! This one is not a magic melon!" he shouted. Up and up and up he climbed some more. When he reached the second melon, he found a second worm inside. "Where's my gold?" he screamed. "It must be in the next melon!"

The greedy man climbed faster, checking each melon as he went, and finding nothing but worms.

Soon, there was only one melon left, and the greedy man climbed toward it as fast as he could.

But the faster he climbed, the faster the plant grew. Up it grew, taller and taller, until finally, the tip of the plant with the biggest, plumpest melon lay on the moon.

"At last! There's my magic melon!" the greedy man shouted.

He didn't notice that below him, the plant was withering and dying. And as he stepped onto the moon, the runners of the dead melon plant fell to earth. He could not return home.

And so it was then, and so it is now. If you go outside on a clear night and look up into the evening sky, and if you look closely, you can still see the face of the greedy man in the moon.

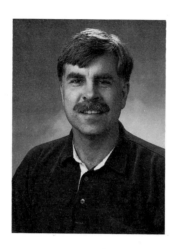

About the Author

Rick Rossiter's interest in storytelling began in 1977 when he was a first-grade teacher. One afternoon, master storyteller Arne Nixon visited his classroom, and by the end of the visit, a warm, magical spell was cast that has lasted to this day.

Rick has been a professional storyteller since 1979. When he finds or writes a story that is special, he tests it on his wife and family: Lee Anne, Jason, Brahm, Rachel, and son-in-law Matt. Rick travels to schools and storytelling festivals throughout the United States. He visits about 175 schools annually, conducting workshops and telling stories in English, Spanish, and American Sign Language for the deaf.

He has received three California Art Council grants, has presented material before the International Reading Association, and has been a Fresno Pacific College Extension instructor. He has recorded two audiocassettes, "Old Time Tellin'" and "When Animals Could Talk." Rick belongs to the National Storytelling Association.

The Greedy Man in the Moon is his first book for Riverbank Press.

The Rossiters live in Lemoore, California.